PUFFIN BOOKS

The WILDEST Day at the Zoo

Alan Rusbridger lives in London with a family that includes a wife, two daughters, a dog called Angus and a cat called Retro. He has forgotten why the cat is called Retro. He also edits the *Guardian*.

Books by Alan Rusbridger

THE COLDEST DAY IN THE ZOO
THE WILDEST DAY AT THE ZOO

ALAN RUSBRIDGER

The WILDEST Day at the Zoo

Illustrated by Ben Cort

PUFFIN

PUFFIN BOOKS

Published by the Penguin Group
Penguin Books Ltd, 80 Strand, London WC2R 0RL, England
Penguin Group (USA) Inc., 375 Hudson Street, New York, New York 10014, USA
Penguin Group (Canada), 10 Alcorn Avenue, Toronto, Ontario, Canada M4V 3B2
(a division of Pearson Penguin Canada Inc.)
Penguin Ireland, 25 St Stephen's Green, Dublin 2, Ireland (a division of Penguin Books Ltd)
Penguin Group (Australia), 250 Camberwell Road, Camberwell, Victoria 3124, Australia
(a division of Pearson Australia Group Pty Ltd)
Penguin Books India Pvt Ltd, 11 Community Centre, Panchsheel Park, New Delhi – 110 017, India
Penguin Group (NZ), cnr Airborne and Rosedale Roads, Albany, Auckland 1310, New Zealand
(a division of Pearson New Zealand Ltd)
Penguin Books (South Africa) (Pty) Ltd, 24 Sturdee Avenue, Rosebank, Johannesburg 2196, South Africa

Penguin Books Ltd, Registered Offices: 80 Strand, London WC2R 0RL, England

www.penguin.com

First published 2005
5

Text copyright © Alan Rusbridger, 2005
Illustrations copyright © Ben Cort, 2005
All rights reserved

The moral right of the author and illustrator has been asserted

Set in Bembo
Made and printed in England by Clays Ltd, St Ives plc

British Library Cataloguing in Publication Data
A CIP catalogue record for this book is available from the British Library

ISBN 0–141–31933–X

To Matthew (in memory of stories past) –
and Molly and Oliver (in memory of stories future)

Chapter One

Mr Raja was bored. He had been the rhino keeper at Melton Meadow Zoo for eight years and he felt like a change. Not a permanent change: he loved his rhino too much to ditch him altogether. But sometimes he couldn't help wondering what it would be like to spend a little time with some other animals.

Maybe just for a day.

So when he got to work that morning Mr Raja knocked on the door of the head keeper, Mr Pickles.

'Excuse me for bothering you,' he said very politely, 'but I've been looking after rhinos for eight years now . . .'

'And you want a change?' asked Mr Pickles.

'Not a permanent change,' said Mr Raja.

'Just for a day?' asked Mr Pickles.

'Er, well, yes,' said Mr Raja, very surprised. 'How did you guess?'

'Because you're the second keeper this morning to come in with the same idea.' Mr Pickles paused for thought for a moment. 'Do you like insects?'

The question took Mr Raja by surprise. He hadn't got much beyond wanting to look after anything but a rhino. He had vaguely been thinking of something more like a tiger than a

grasshopper or a beetle. But he didn't wish to be rude, so he nodded again.

'Insects, er, yes,' he mumbled. 'I love them.'

'Excellent,' said Mr Pickles. 'Because Miss Ingleby told me she also wants a change, so you could swap. In fact, why don't you all swap for a day? Can't have our keepers getting bored.'

And that was how all the keepers in Melton Meadow Zoo ended up looking after each other's animals for the day.

Chapter Two

The following Monday – All Change Day – Mr Raja leapt out of bed early and set off for the zoo with a bounce in his step. He wondered whether his rhino would miss him for the day. No one else had ever looked after him.

Mr Raja met Miss Ingleby at the Insect House, shook hands, wished her luck with the rhino and went in.

It was quite dark inside the Insect House and very quiet. In fact, for a while he couldn't see any insects at all. Then he walked around the room peering into various glass tanks with labels – 'Bugs', 'Lice', 'Fleas' and so on – and he shuddered.

Oh dear, thought Mr Raja to himself. *I'm not sure I like the idea of those.* He had rather been hoping for

some friendly sounding insects like
dragonflies or lacewings or butterflies.

Just then he heard a tiny scraping
sound and saw something small and
black scuttling along the floor. He was

just about to stamp on it when he remembered where he was. It was a cockroach all right, but he couldn't tell whether it was a common cockroach, which had wandered in off the street, or whether it was some rare cockroach that had escaped from a glass tank.

He peered at the cockroach. The cockroach peered back, a bit crossly, or so Mr Raja thought. So he went to the keeper's office and returned with a tumbler, a magnifying glass and one of Miss Ingleby's books about insects. He placed the tumbler over the cockroach and got down on his hands and knees to have an even closer look.

He was just flicking through the pages trying to decide whether his little friend was a tawny cockroach or a dusky cockroach when he heard Mr Pickles clearing his throat right behind him.

'I just wondered . . .' began Mr Pickles, but he got no further. Mr Raja was so startled to hear a human voice in the dark silence of the Insect House that he jumped up, knocking over the nearest glass tank.

Crash! went the glass, splintering all over the floor. And then there was an almighty buzzing sound as whatever it was inside the tank escaped and started, well, buzzing.

'Don't worry, Mr Pickles, all is under control,' said Mr Raja, bending down to pick up the name label to find out what on earth could be making that irritating buzz, which was rapidly becoming more like an angry roar.

Mr Raja felt faint as he read the label.

Big red letters spelled W-A-S-P-S.

Wasps!

'Oh dear,' said Mr Raja.

Then disaster struck. A well–built queen wasp, extremely put out at all the commotion, took aim at Mr Pickles's ample bottom and sank her sting into it.

'Aaaaaargh!' cried Mr Pickles.

'Oh dear!' said Mr Raja again.

Mr Pickles swiped the wasp off his bottom, and it flew off and settled on a nearby wall. Mr Raja picked up Miss Ingleby's book on insects . . . and advanced on the queen wasp, intent on crushing it to a pulp.

'Stop!' cried Mr Pickles. 'Always remember – we're zookeepers. It's our duty to look after the animals, no matter what.'

Just then the queen wasp flew off, did an elegant loop-the-loop and landed on Mr Pickles's forehead. By now the wasp had taken a real dislike to the two intruders: one kept shouting, and the other had attempted to squash her with his large book. Where, she wondered, was her regular keeper? And so, just for good measure, she stung Mr Pickles again – right in the middle of his nose.

'Grrrrr!' groaned Mr Pickles, snatching the book from Mr Raja and closing in on the queen wasp, who had now come to rest on a windowpane. He suddenly forgot about his duty to look after the animals. He was set on revenge.

Thud! went the book against the window, narrowly missing the queen wasp, who had seen it coming. Then *crash!* as the windowpane broke, shattering the glass into a thousand pieces.

The sound of breaking glass sent the wasps into a frenzy. They clustered

into two swarms, one of which flew straight out of the window and was last seen heading in the general direction of Melton Meadow high street.

The other swarm gathered over the head of poor Mr Pickles, who by now was really quite hot and bothered. He took one look at the buzzing cloud and ran screaming from the Insect House, followed by Mr Raja, approximately 300 angry wasps and at least one tawny cockroach.

Chapter Three

Meanwhile, in the Rhino House, Miss Ingleby was deep in study. She had no idea of the mayhem in the Insect House. Instead, she was reading her favourite book, *The*

Complete Encyclopedia of Insects.

The huge white rhino had been asleep in the corner of his pen ever since she had arrived, so she thought she could use the time to learn a bit more about her lifelong passion.

Miss Ingleby loved books, especially books about insects. The books she read could not agree on how many insects there were on the planet. Some said there were one million different species, while others said there could be as many as ten million. Whatever the number, Miss Ingleby knew she would never get bored.

On the table in front of her – beside *The Complete Encyclopedia of Insects* – was a beetle.

Now, Miss Ingleby felt a little guilty about taking this beetle with her, because the zoo rules said you should never take an animal out of its enclosure. But Miss Ingleby had a special reason. The beetle was a rhinoceros beetle, and she thought it was about time that the rhinoceros beetle met a real rhinoceros.

Miss Ingleby turned to the rhinoceros-beetle page in *The Complete Encyclopedia of Insects.*

'Rhinoceros beetles are the world's strongest animals,' she read. She glanced across at the mammoth rhino snoring a few metres away, and back at the little black bug on the desk in front of her and smiled at the thought that her little beetle was stronger than that enormous great bruiser.

Miss Ingleby decided to make the huge snoring white rhino some breakfast, so that when he woke up he would have something nice and welcoming to eat. She had no idea how much to feed the animal. Her insects were usually happy nibbling a leaf or a berry for breakfast. And lunch and tea, come to that.

She looked in the book on the shelf called *Rhino Care: All You Need to Know*. She found the food section and read that the slumbering hulk in front of her would be expecting more than twenty-seven kilograms of hay and four and a half kilograms of pellets plus an assortment of dry white potatoes, carrots, cabbages and two or three loaves of bread. All in one day.

'Dear me!' said Miss Ingleby. 'What a lot of food!' And she made a note to enquire whether the loaves should be sliced or unsliced.

She thought it would be a good idea to put the rhinoceros beetle in a box while she made the rhino his breakfast. But where was the rhinoceros beetle? He wasn't on the table and she couldn't see him anywhere on the floor.

The Rhino House was rather dark, and quite warm, so Miss Ingleby opened the door to get a bit more light into the room and went back to inspect the rhino, who was just showing signs of waking up. First one enormous eye – the size of a tennis ball – opened, and then the other. Then the animal's left ear began to twitch. It was the biggest ear Miss Ingleby had ever seen. It looked like a football that had been sawn in half and then squashed into the shape of a shell.

Twitch, twitch, twitch, it went. Miss Ingleby looked more closely. Twitch, twitch.

She peered right into the ear. There, to her astonishment, she saw the rhinoceros beetle scuttling around in the darkness, making himself quite at home. Miss Ingleby felt a bit panicky. She had certainly wanted the rhinoceros beetle to meet the rhinoceros, but she had never imagined he would want to set up home in his ear.

Very gingerly she leant over the rhino and tried to reach inside the giant shell to scoop up the beetle. But the beetle was having none of it. He waved his long claws around in the air, which had the effect of tickling the bristles on the inside of the rhino's ear.

This was most irritating for the rhino. His ear twitched again. The beetle — who now thought this was a rather good game — gave the inside of the ear a playful scratch.

Twitch.

Scratch.

Twitch.

Scratch . . .

Twitch . . .

. . . Scratch

. . . Scratch

. . . and then . . .

CHARGE!

The rhino lost patience with

whatever was doing ballet in his ear. He saw the open door, groped to his feet, pawed the ground . . . and then he lowered his head and charged out of the door.

Now a rhino may be big, lumbering and not very elegant, but when it goes, it goes. And this rhino went.

CHARGE!

Out through the Rhino House door. Out past the ice cream stall. Out past Mr Pickles and his swarm of wasps. Out past the ticket office.

He was last seen heading off at forty-five miles per hour in the general direction of Melton Meadow high street. Which was, strictly speaking, breaking the speed limit.

Chapter Four

Over in the Chimpanzee House
Mrs Brock, the polar-bear keeper,
was reading the instructions left for
her by Mr Chisel, the chimp keeper.

Breakfast it said on a scribbled piece

of paper.

Three oranges (sometimes refused)

Six apples

Six bananas

Half a loaf of raisin bread

Quarter of a head of cabbage

Two pints of milk

But at this point a young chimp leapt on to Mrs Brock's shoulders as if from nowhere and ripped the instructions out of her hands. The chimp kissed Mrs Brock on the cheek, ruffled her hair, tore up the feeding instructions and ran off, hooting with laughter.

Mrs Brock frowned. Her bears
might be big and dangerous, but they
were generally very well behaved. She
could see she was going to have to
lick this lot into shape.

Mrs Brock tried to remember what was on the list for breakfast, but she couldn't remember anything except *Three oranges (sometimes refused)*. So she took out her mobile phone to ring Mr Chisel, who had helpfully offered to give advice if she needed it.

'Mr Chisel?' said Mrs Brock. 'I just
wanted a spot of . . .'

But she got no further. With a
big swoosh a chimp swung past

her right shoulder, one arm clinging
to a rope as the other arm swiped the
phone away from her ear.

He shrieked with delight. He hadn't had this much fun since he'd snatched a wig off the bald head of a visiting keeper from Belgium.

'Give me my phone back!' shouted Mrs Brock. But the chimp swung over the pool and dropped the phone with a big splash into the water (which is what he'd done with the Belgian visitor's wig). *The old tricks are the best ones*, he reflected to himself, chuckling.

'Really!' spluttered Mrs Brock, rather exasperated as one chimp stole her handbag and started rifling through the contents while another pulled at her shoelaces and tried to eat them.

Mrs Brock remembered that milk had been on Mr Chisel's list, so with some difficulty (because another chimp was now trying to pull her trousers off) she limped across to the food store and poured three cups of milk. The chimp let go of her trousers and took a big mouthful of milk.

'There now,' said Mrs Brock severely. 'Perhaps that'll calm you down a bit.'

The chimp looked moderately calm for all of five seconds. And then he squirted the milk straight in Mrs Brock's astonished face with a shriek that could be heard halfway to Melton Paxford.

Chapter Five

'Are you having trouble?' Mr Chisel walked through the door with a worried expression. He suspected there was a problem when the line suddenly went dead in the middle of his phone call with Mrs Brock. He took one look at the milky, trembling figure in front of him and realized that things were every bit as bad as he feared.

'Yes, I am,' said Mrs Brock furiously. 'Say what you like about my bears, but at least they have decent manners.'

Mr Chisel looked at Mrs Brock, mopping a big blob of milk from her spectacles. And he looked at the naughty chimp, hugging himself with laughter on the ground. And Mr Chisel was suddenly overcome with a terrible urge to laugh as well.

The urge welled up from deep inside his tummy until it exploded in his throat and he let out a strange little yelp of glee. And then another, and then another. The sight of Mr Chisel squealing set all the other chimps off laughing even harder.

'Outrageous!' growled Mrs Brock. 'I've never been so insulted in all my –'

But as she turned to the door – intent on marching off to complain to Mr Pickles – Mrs Brock was confronted by the sight of the biggest polar bear you have ever seen, lumbering slowly through the door.

'And what,' asked Mrs Brock menacingly, 'is *he* doing here?'

'Er,' mumbled Mr Chisel, who had

suddenly stopped feeling like he was about to burst with laughter. 'Er, I suppose I must have left the door open.'

'I suppose you did,' said Mrs Brock sharply.

'Is it true what they say about polar bears?' asked Mr Chisel, backing away from the bear. He was waving a banana at the advancing bear, a banana being the only object to hand.

'What?' said Mrs Brock.

'That they, er, hunt . . .' Mr Chisel's voice tailed off.

'Human beings?' asked Mrs Brock. 'Only very ill-mannered human beings.'

Mr Chisel gulped. 'Er, quite,' he said. 'Do you think if I offered this bear – this charming bear – my banana, he might realize that I am really quite well mannered?'

'Polar bears do not eat bananas,' said Mrs Brock. 'As you would know, if you had read the helpful note I left for you.'

Mr Chisel swallowed hard. 'Ah, yes, so you did,' he mumbled. 'Four and a half kilograms of raw meat, that was it.'

'And one kilogram each of butterfish and mackerel,' added Mrs Brock.

'Yes, so it was,' said Mr Chisel, who was now feeling very sorry for himself. 'How could I forget?'

But just then a baby chimp – bored by all this grown-up conversation and lack of laughter – decided to cheer things up by jumping on top of the bear and tweaking his left ear.

The bear let out a low, grumbling, rolling growl and rose up on two legs. He was now three metres high and, in Mr Chisel's considered opinion, not at all funny.

The baby chimp also realized that none of the other chimps was laughing any more. So he jumped off the bear's back and scuttled out the door. The polar bear followed.

It is a little known fact that, if it so wishes, a polar bear can reach speeds of up to thirty-four miles per hour. And so it was that at least two animals broke the speed limit in Melton Meadow that morning as the polar bear also headed towards the high street.

Chapter Six

Mr Pickles had by now managed —
with Miss Ingleby's help — to escape
the swarm of wasps and decided to
make a tour of the rest of the zoo to
see how things were going. He was —

so far – blissfully ignorant of the other escaped animals. He had put on some ointment to ease the wasp stings, and was feeling a tiny bit more cheerful.

First he popped into the Snake House, where Mrs Mills – who normally worked in the Mouse House – was working for the day.

He found her trembling with anger.

'Mr Pickles!' she exploded when she saw him. 'I have just been feeding this anaconda.'

'Ye-ees?' said Mr Pickles gently.

'I was just opening the door to his

box, thinking he'd have some cereal or toast or fruit for breakfast. And then I read in the instructions what he actually eats.'

'Ye-ees?' said Mr Pickles gingerly.

'Mice!' screamed Mrs Mills. 'This snake is fed on mice!'

'Er, which snake?' asked Mr Pickles nervously, eyeing up what appeared to be an empty glass box.

'That horrible, slithery, mouse-eating ...'

Mrs Mills fell silent as she, too, realized the box was empty.

Out of the corner of his eye Mr Pickles saw what looked like a length of green rope sliding out of the door.

'Oh dear!' he sighed, not for the first time that morning. Mr Pickles followed the snake – although, secretly, he had no idea how to catch an anaconda.

Luckily for Mr Pickles there was no opportunity to show off his lack of snake-catching skills, as he was immediately greeted by a scene of utter mayhem. A dozen extremely

dishevelled and anxious keepers came running towards Mr Pickles, and animals were now running everywhere – including two small marmosets eating ice-cream cones, and a very slithery anaconda.

Mr Pickles was distracted at this point, however, by a young chimpanzee, who crept up behind him, snatched at his hand and ran off at high speed with his keys, cackling at his own cleverness.

'Oh dear!' said Mr Pickles again as he realized that the mischievous young chimp now had the master key to all the cages in the zoo. He walked back to his office, where, with shaking hands, he picked up the phone and dialled 999.

'Emergency services,' said a voice on the other end. 'Which service do you require — police, ambulance or fire brigade?'

'All of them!' groaned Mr Pickles, his head sinking into his hand.

A policeman came on the line.

'It's Mr Pickles, head keeper at Melton Meadow Zoo,' said Mr Pickles. 'There's been a slight, er, accident. Well, actually, more than one . . .'

'What kind of accident?' asked the policeman.

'Well, er, a number of, um, animals, have, er, escaped.'

'Escaped!' exclaimed the policeman. 'Where to?'

'Um, well, as far as I know they are heading for Melton Meadow High Street,' said Mr Pickles.

'And exactly which animals,' asked the policeman slowly, 'have escaped?'

'Yes, well,' said Mr Pickles, consulting a list which Mr Raja had just pushed in front of him, 'one swarm of angry wasps . . .'

'One swarm of angry wasps,' repeated the policeman, writing it down as he went.

' . . . one rhinoceros, up to twenty chimpanzees, a polar bear . . .'

'Not so fast, I have to write all this down,' said the policeman.

' . . . and an anaconda.'

'Is that "ana" with an "a", or "ano" with an "o"?' asked the policeman.

'Does it matter?' asked Mr Pickles, suddenly panicking. 'All you need to know about an anaconda is that it's seven and a half metres long, wraps itself around its victims and then crushes them to death.'

There was a long silence at the other end of the phone.

'And where did you say this ana-whatsit was?' asked the policeman.

'I told you, they were all last seen heading for Melton Meadow High Street,' said Mr Pickles. 'Oh, and I've just heard that the chimpanzee has unlocked the door to the lion house . . .'

Mr Pickles heard the sound of a phone being dropped at the other end, and then the line went dead.

Chapter Seven

'Right, you lot,' shouted Mr Pickles to the keepers, who had by now all gathered in his office. 'What are we waiting for?'

The keepers jumped into four vans

and headed off for the high street, grabbing whatever gloves, nets, ropes and tempting bananas they could lay their hands on at a minute's notice.

As they got close to the high street they heard 'nee-nor . . . nee-nor . . . nee-nor' as police cars, fire engines and ambulances raced in from all directions.

And then they saw big green army
trucks rumbling down the hill from
Melton Sodbury. And a helicopter.
And then a tank.

'Oh no!' said Mr Pickles to himself. 'This is all my fault. How could I have been such a fool?'

'Oh no!' said Mr Raja to himself. 'This was all my rotten idea.'

'Oh no!' said Miss Ingleby to herself. 'I'm completely to blame.'

But by the time they reached the town hall Mr Pickles had pulled himself together and sent the keepers out to catch their animals in double-quick time.

Mr Raja soon found his rhino, which had leapt into the town fountains in an attempt to flood out whatever it was that was now doing vigorous press-ups in his ear. The trick had succeeded in dislodging the rhinoceros beetle, and the rhino had begun to enjoy his cooling bath,

posing politely for pictures whenever a local resident asked nicely.

Then Miss Ingleby came back to her van with her wasps all safely netted up, and a rather damp and sorry-for-itself rhinoceros beetle, which she had found trying to clamber out of a puddle near the town fountain.

Miss Syllabub, the snake keeper, found the anaconda near some workmen, who were laying drains in Oliver Street. The giant snake was pretending to be a drainpipe in the hope that a luckless workman would try to pick him up. His plan was to coil himself around the unsuspecting workman and have him for tea.

The plan worked – up to a point. A workman was indeed fooled into mistaking him for a drainpipe. In fact, he had just drawn a line on the anaconda's back and was about to saw

him in half when Miss Syllabub ran
up, panting.

'Stop!' she cried. 'It's not a drainpipe, it's a snake!'

'Oh yeah?' scoffed the workman. 'Then how come it smells of drains?'

At this, the anaconda, who had never been so insulted, let out a violent hiss. The workman dropped his saw and ran for his life. And Miss Syllabub had to speak to the anaconda very severely (while reassuring him about his excellent personal hygiene) before she could entice him back into the van.

The chimpanzees — all seventeen of them — headed straight for Mr Green's fruit and veg stall, much to the astonishment of Mr Green, who had run it for twenty-five years without encountering anything more exciting than a golden retriever with three legs. Mr Green started to give each chimp a banana, which was thoughtful of him, but — so far as the chimps were concerned — only a start. Within minutes they had stripped the stall of cabbage, celery sticks and grapes and were having a whale of a time pelting each other — and any unlucky passers-by — with potatoes.

Mr Chisel groaned when he saw them behaving so badly. There was only one

 thing for it: his secret weapon − chocolate digestive biscuits. So he bought an entire box of them from the astonished shopkeeper next door and started bribing the chimps one at a time. One by one they dropped their food and ammunition and followed Mr Chisel into the van. Fourteen packets later the chimps had all calmed down and were back in the van, where three of the greedier ones were duly sick. All over Mr Chisel.

Mrs Brock happened to be passing

the van door just as the last chimp threw up in Mr Chisel's lap and she couldn't resist a quiet little chuckle at Mr Chisel's expense. But not too much of a chuckle, because she had not yet found her polar bear.

She eventually tracked him down in the fishmonger's, where the bear was sitting in the middle of the floor, helping himself to a nice selection of salmon, cod, prawns, plaice, trout and anything else he could lay his paws on.

Mrs Brock knew that, for a polar bear, there was only one thing better

than a fish feast — and that was an ice lolly. She had sometimes given the bear lollies on very hot days, and knew that even the sight of them reduced him to a quivering jelly of pleasure. So she bought a dozen orange lollies and — one by one — used them to coax him back to the waiting van.

The last to arrive was Mr Leaf, having finally tracked down his lion, who had walked straight through the front door of the town hall and into the mayor's office. Mr Leaf thought it was because the lion considered himself to be the king of the animals, and so it was only appropriate to visit the mayor. The mayor thought it was more likely that the lion had smelled the juicy hamburger with melted cheese and big fries which he had just bought, and which he was wisely handing over to the lion just as Mr Leaf showed up.

By lunchtime on All Change Day everything was back to normal. The police, fire brigade, ambulances and army had all gone back to their bases; the animals were all back in their normal houses with their normal

keepers; and Mr Pickles had gone home for a little lie-down.

It had been the wildest day at the zoo.

The one thing he knew would never, ever, EVER happen again was All Change Day at Melton Meadow Zoo.